Copyright © 2025 by Millasia Archangel

Music Copyright © Howard Harper Barnes

Cover by Millasia Archangel

Scripture quotations taken from The Holy Bible, *New International Version*®, *NIV*®. Copyright © 1973, 1978, 1984, 2011 by Biblica, Inc.® Used by permission. All rights reserved worldwide.

All rights reserved. This book or parts thereof may not be reproduced in any form, stored in any retrieval system, or transmitted in any form by any means—electronic, mechanical, photocopy, recording, or otherwise—without prior written and signed permission of the author, except as provided by United States of America copyright law and fair use.

ISBN 979-8-9924119-1-1

Printed in the United States of America

First Edition

The anthology you are about to read is an adaptation of the Exodus story. The biblical account of Moses can be found in the book of Exodus.

To my God,

The God of Israel,

His people, and His prophet,

my mom.

INSTRUCTIONS

Instructions

This is your encounter, and you should treat it as such. He is the true author of this anthology. In consecration and isolation, this work was written whilst the musical compositions, recorded below each act, sounded. Thus, consecrate yourself. Isolate yourself. Listen to each composition — all of which are composed by Howard Harper Barnes — once prior to reading. He will hear it, and He will come to you. Read according to how it is written.

The Faintest Touch

Anna's Log

The Investigation

Refined Enlightenment

The Watchers

Underlying Truth

Forests in Mist

To Boldly Go

I Will Come Back for You

The Faintest Touch

ACT I
BEFORE DAWN
THE FAINTEST TOUCH

I: *Zipporah*

Moses and Zipporah sit, the candlelight burnishing the fabric of their tent. An array of reds, browns, and oranges that weave the colors of the Midianite desert together. In His original intention, they sit, before Moses tends to her father's flock.

When I see him, I see beauty.

Or perhaps it is my love for my love that obscures what is not beautiful and makes it so.

But then, I watch the candle warm the red undertones of his bronze skin and betray the hair strands that run brown.

I take in his irises and the prominent bridge of his nose that balances the craftsmanship of his face.

God's craftsmanship.

And I realize that my conditional love cannot conceal what is not beautiful and make it so, but God's anointing can.

And here, in our tent, in the hours between night and morning... where time doesn't feel quite real, the anointing is as present as we are.

Looking up from his hands that hold mine, I confer, "I think I have my answer." He mouths more than says, "I have mine too."

"When I see you... I see beauty.

Could it be my love for my love that obscures what is not beautiful and makes it so?

Perhaps...

But as I watch the candle warm the red undertones of your bronze skin, betraying the hair strands that run brown.

As I take in your irises, poured pure for me, and the prominent bridge of your nose that balances the craftsmanship of your face —

God's craftmanship.

I realize that my conditional love cannot conceal what God's anointing can.

And here... now... in the hours between night and morning where time doesn't feel quite real, the anointing is as present as we are."

Tears gather but his eyes do not run from mine.

"When I see you... I see your first love.

He who is before me.

He who is after.

In prayer, I feel a heart that yearns... even faints, to be near Him.

Elegant hands that seek consecration to be in the court of the Lord... without the praise... without the recognition... just to be seen by Him.

But I.

I praise you for it.

I praise your heart and mind as masterpieces burned clean by His touch.

If only you understood.

If you fell in love with Him and His fellowship,

He fell for you first."

Tears gather and fall for what he speaks only God Himself could know. The longing in his eyes reaches out beyond flesh and takes hold of something so compelling, I sob.

Hurt and healed all at once.

ACT II
THE ENCOUNTER
ANNA'S LOG

II: *Moses*

Flames, blue like that of indicolite, burn beautifully, quietly, in the darkness surrounding it. Catching... capturing his attention. Branch and leaf remain. Fascinated, he brushes his fingertips against the presence of God.

His holiness withdraws breath from body, lighting the throat aflame.

His voice calls out to the spirit that cries out to the living God... "Moses."

"Lord."

"I am."

"I have seen the misery of my people.

I have heard them, and I am concerned about their suffering.

So, I have come down."

Away from the natural, aware but absent, I see His feet... unblemished... in sandals without fray... walking upon white sand.

Leading.

His heel rising, the impression beneath unrevealed.

The tassel, a blur amidst His pronouncement.

> "I am sending you to Pharaoh to bring them up and out of Egypt."

I writhe.

> "But Lord, who am I?"

> "The Son of Jochebed. I will be with you."

> "... suppose I go. What should I say is your name?"

"I am who I am."

Generational adoration from the grave — mantle upon mantle upon mantle — takes hold of me.

My spirit, it knows Him.

My spirit has already seen The Holy One of Israel on the throne.

There, in the courtroom of Heaven, listening.

Answering.

Delivering.

A still God who moves.

His heart, the lot cast to slaves, because chained hands are the only ones open to receiving it.

Though things were not meant to be this way.

A thoughtful heart.

Eyes that behold righteousness and justice, undefined by man.

Lips that will not lie to me.

Hands that will not take His love from me.

Your heavenly hand, once reluctantly still, rises...

fingers outstretched.

Your feet,

a lamp for my own.

The Shepherd of the Shepherd.

ACT III
ARRIVAL IN EGYPT
THE INVESTIGATION

III: *Moses*

Moses, robed in the most ebon form of olivine, stands next to Aaron, lissome with skin the color of sand. Behind and between is Zipporah. Carved columns of gold cascade the throne room, reaching a height light cannot. Darkness hovers over their engravings... the writings of priests' allure, almost seduce, the things that reside here. Palm leaves peak out, reflecting the light, tinted larimar blue, coming down from above Pharaoh's throne.

It passes over him but what sits is far from man.

Something... animalistic and demoniacal studies me, even speaks, "Who is the Lord that I should obey him?"

"... you know who He is."

"And if you do not let us take this journey to offer sacrifices unto

Him, He may strike us with plagues.

Or even the sword."

"Plagues?

Look, I do not know the Lord,

nor will I let Israel go.

They are…

my slaves after all."

Israelite men gather too closely, the white of their waist coverings blending together. A chosen people… amber and angles. Magnetic to the eye that admires and the one that abhors.

"Moses. Aaron. Why are you taking the people away from their labor?"

Regarding his officials, he orders, "Have them get back to work."

Several leave their post; black and red beads swaying across their demon revealed faces.

"Pharaoh." I say, stepping forward.

"I think I have heard enough from you.

Take your wife and your brother and go."

ACT IV
TO BE HIS
REFINED
ENLIGHTENMENT

IV: *Moses*

*D*efeat pursues me.

It is after my body.

After whom it is you say I am.

Relentlessly... and without mercy, I am proven inferior and inadequate.

Defeat pursues me. All because I am pursuing you.

It is after the pen in my hand.

After my praise for you.

I am constantly fighting to stand on ground you have placed me on.

Fighting only to fail.

Defeat finds its way even into the answered prayer.

And yet I pursue...

I run...

I chase after you.

My glory is stolen, so you robe me in yours.

Unseen by man

because you too

are unseen.

"Why, Lord, why have you brought trouble on these people?

I spoke in your Name and now, their workload has been doubled.

They are worse off than before.

Have I misheard you?"

...

"Have I misheard you?"

...

"I am the Lord.

I appeared to your forefathers as God Almighty,

but by my Name... the Lord, I did not make myself fully known.

I will free them from being slaves.

I will redeem them with mighty acts of judgement.

I will take them as my own.

And I will be their God.

I am the Lord."

ACT V
THE PLAGUE OF BLOOD

V: *Moses*

On the Nile bank, mist dims the morning sun and reeds, tall and bending, break beneath their feet.

"Pharaoh!

Has the Lord not commanded you to let His people go?

He has, but you have not listened.

Instead, you say, 'Who is the Lord that I should obey him?'

By this, you will know."

I kneel to watch the water speculatively.

...

"Aaron, you will stretch out your hand over the waters of Egypt —

the narrowest of rivers and the widest of canals,

over every hidden pond and all the reservoirs —

> so that they will turn into blood.
>
> But first, take your staff and strike the Nile."

Red ripples and spreads...

darkens,

thickens,

steals breath from the gills of fish.

The smell of copper rises

as do I.

> "Blood will be everywhere in Egypt!
>
> The fish will die, and the river will stink.
>
> You say, 'Who is the Lord that I should obey him?'
>
> This is He."

ACT VI
THE PLAGUE OF FROGS
THE WATCHERS

VI: *Moses*

Overrun. The throne room is overrun. Hundreds... thousands of eggs float in clusters... in strings through bloody water. In the shallow basin of kneading troughs and domes of ovens, empty of bread, frogs... warted, red, and deformed... lie. Outside, officials and frogs watch him... eyes protruding, limbs folded underneath.

The gold, the leaves, the pride

has dulled.

There is only the ribbitting.

"Pray to the Lord to take the frogs away... and I will let your people go to offer sacrifices unto him."

"I leave you the honor of setting the time for me to pray."

"Tomorrow."

"It will be as you say.

The frogs will leave, except for those that remain in the Nile."

A nod of dismissal is given but no relief is felt.

ACT VII
THE PLAGUE OF GNATS, FLIES, AND BOILS
UNDERLYING TRUTH

VII:

A rippling, the same as in the Nile, lifts dust from the ground. Dust stills and gathers for all to see.

Deep in Pharaoh's left ear...

    "For every drop of sweat, a gnat will be sent forth to bombard.

        To harass.

        An incessant buzzing."

He groans, covering his ears in vain.

His breath.

The finger of God points dense swarms of flies in the direction in which they should go. Into Pharaoh's palace... his bedroom... onto his bed.

His breath.

Handfuls of black soot are tossed into the air.

A crying out from people and animals.

Boils, purple and tender, fill with pus.

Fester,

spread,

cluster,

rupture.

His breath.

ACT VIII
THE CONFRONTATION
FORESTS IN MIST

VIII: *Pharaoh*

*W*ithin the palace...

The outline of the columns, I cannot see.

Darkness swallows my vision,

His voice, my mind.

I cannot see.

My surroundings are larger, further

than they should be.

The lights around the altar will not burn.

He has closed the sky.

I saw it.

"All I have done and yet..."

"And yet?"

"You do not know that there is no one like me in all the earth. For by now, I could have struck you and your people with a plague that could have wiped you off of it.

You still set yourself against my people."

"... you be with them – if I let them go!"

ACT IX
A PEOPLE HE WOULD LEAVE THE THRONE FOR.

IX:

*A*n east wind, great and powerful, blows across the land all day and all night, bringing locusts by morning. But the Lord was not in the wind. Darkness spreads across the sky, one that could be felt, but the Lord was not in the darkness. It surrounds Him; righteousness and justice are the foundation of His throne.

At a table, lit by a melting candle, Moses writes, 'Fire goes before him and consumes his foes on every side.'

On the floor of a cave, Elijah writes of a wind that tore mountains apart, and after this wind, an earthquake. And after this earthquake, a fire. And after this fire, a gentle whisper.

During the rule of Belshazzar, Daniel writes, 'As I looked, thrones were set in place, and the Ancient of Days took his seat. His throne was flaming with fire, and its wheels were all ablaze. A river of fire was flowing, coming out from before him.'

From heaven on high,

He looks down and sees me.

His hair, pure wool.

Not a knot or tangle in sight.

From heaven on high,

green eyes, resemblant of jewel,

looks down and sees me.

There is no word for the beauty of His features.

Bronze hands,

capable of so much,

usher for a chariot.

Egyptian men regard Moses as he speaks to Israel,

"The animals you choose must be year old males without defect.

Slaughter them at twilight.

Eat and do not leave any of it till morning.

With your cloak tucked into your belt,

sandals on your feet,

and staff in your hand,

eat it in haste.

It is the Lord's Passover."

ACT X
CROSSING THE SEA
TO BOLDLY GO

X: *God*

With my finger, I draw the sea back.

It folds as a curtain would,

sounds of the earth cracking,

reaches the ears of those miles away.

Birds flock from branches in fear.

Thunder and earthquake are quiet.

Quiet compared to the sea and the creatures within

writhing at my command.

The sky bleeds red above.

In a neighboring nation, a man rises in disbelief.

And defeat still pursues.

So I throw it into confusion.

Per my order,

angels, the mighty ones who do my bidding,

and my heavenly hosts

who carry out my will,

shoot forth arrows, jamming the wheels of the Egyptians' chariots.

When the last of mine has crossed,

I release the sea,

leaving no impression.

ACT XI
THE REUNIFICATION PART I
I WILL COME BACK FOR YOU

XI:

At some point, Moses and Zipporah agreed that it was best for her to return to her father's house, Jethro. Serving as judge for the people, being the one to stand between them and the Lord took its toll. This is their reunification.

A spring on the mountainside, lit by lamps of oil, awaits Zipporah. Its waterfall foams white, spreads blue, edges green from algae. The yellow fronds of palm trees, planted long ago in preparation for her arrival, lean over the water.

Moses' young aide, Joshua, who escorted her here, speaks up, "This spring has been set aside for you. Your husband, he says, 'I will be there in the hour between night and morning where time doesn't feel quite real.'"

And he was.

In view of her, he shouts, "Is that my love?"

At the sound of his voice, her husband's voice, she is on her feet. Weightless and smothered, she is embraced as is he. Her fingers nervously jump from his hair unto his arms, lips parting to speak, but they are his.

After they kiss, he keeps her hand close over his heart, telling her something inaudible to the audience. They share moments unshared for well over an hour before washing.

ACT XII
THE REUNIFICATION
PART II
THE FAINTEST TOUCH

XII: *Zipporah*

Unrobed of all but a sleeveless tunic… and overgrown hair that hasn't seen shears in I don't know how long, he takes in my face.

Moses

Unrobed of all but a black, long sleeve garment... the moonlight catches the water within her hair and about her collarbone, I see her sacrifice.

His spirit moves on the water...

amidst me...

beneath her touch.

Zipporah

It is not sex.

It is not even making love.

For it articulates,

I want to be loved as you have loved me.

Held as you have held me.

Displayed as your masterpiece.

Hidden as your treasure.

Let it be hard for you to be apart from me.

It is in your nature to love and forgive.

And your heart is cast.

I want some part of you unwritten. Untold.

I want your trust.

Year after year, let me earn your trust, show you my fidelity.

Drench me in such consecration, the sight of it grieves you.

For you are reminded of your original intention for man.

Be bold for me that I may be bold for you.

And in all that I ask, I am.

ACKNOWLEDGEMENTS

The work which you have read is finished. Every word absent from these pages is in your hands.

I am not a finished work. My heart is not a finished work. The Lord is still speaking. Disciplining. Teaching. I am still in His hands.

Humility is a fragile thing. It is quite simple to say I do not desire the praise or the adoration that comes along with loving Him out loud. It is another for my heart to follow and reflect that. To be exalted is innate to human nature but I want to be free. Free from the desire itself to be exalted.

So, my dear reader, I have one request. Allow me to pursue. To run. To chase after Him. Without your praise. Without your adoration. Allow Him to display me as His masterpiece but hide me as His treasure.

AUTHOR PHOTO BY URSULA WILLIAMS

MILLASIA ARCHANGEL is the author of *The Author of the Author*. She graduated from Northwestern State University with a Bachelor of Science in Biology. She began writing *The Author of the Author* during her last year of university. She likes the arts of the mind, midnight wine in white blouses, and books.

For more information, write Millasia at

@millasiaarchangelofficial@gmail.com

Or on Instagram

@millasiaarchangelofficial

Made in the USA
Columbia, SC
18 April 2025